A Really, Really, Scary MONSTER STORY !

Written by
Rebecca Blume

Illustrations by Jeanette Koji

A REALLY, REALLY, SCARY MONSTER STORY !

Written by Rebecca Blume

Especially For Taylor Sheridan
On the Ocassion of Her Fifth Birthday May 7, 1998

Illustrations by Jeanette Koji

First Edition

Published by Liberty Artists Management
Catskill, New York, USA

Library Of Congress Catalog Number 2006924798

ISBN 0-9785427-0-3

If you can't find this book at your local bookstore, visit us and place your order at

LibertyArtists.com
31 Liberty Street
Catskill, NY 12414

Printed in Hong Kong

Long ago, a family of monsters was said to live in a forest outside a small farming village. Everyone knew it because their parents had told them.

"Don't go near the glen," people whispered. "Especially at night! It's haunted." And then they would shake their heads and shiver and make funny noises, like, "Oooooooo!"

Which frightened the children.

A little girl once asked her father why.

"Because monsters live there," he said. "Big, hairy monsters, with long, sharp fingernails they never clean, that they use to cut people open. Squish! With smelly, matted hair they never wash or comb, and big, yellow teeth they never brush. And their breath smells real bad. Oooooooo!"

"Did anyone ever see the monsters?"

"Yes," he said, "and they were all eaten up! Oooooooo!" he said again, shivering.

"I'm not afraid of monsters. If a monster tried to eat me up, I'd ock him good, and he'd never try to eat any children again!" she aid, shaking her little fist.

"Just don't go near the forest," warned her father, kissing her oodnight and turning off the light, because she as a brave little girl, and not aid of the dark.

Early the next morning, while her rents were sleeping, she quietly left the use to see for herself if the monsters ere real.

She crossed the meadows and soon came to the edge of the forest

It was very dark. The deeper she went into the forest, the darker it got.

as dark as the blackest night. She walked slowly along the path...

... feeling her way, step by step.

Suddenly, something grabbed her by the hair. She screamed and pulled away, but it held on tight. “Let me go!” she screamed! She screamed louder, “Let go of me! Let me go!” She turned and tried to kick the monster, but it was invisible. She tried to run, but the monster held on. Its long, sharp fingernails dug into her scalp. She pulled and pulled until she finally broke loose. She looked around for the monster, but it was gone. She was alone. Only branches swayed silently over the path. She touched her hair and screamed again! The monster’s fingers were still in her hair!

“Let me go!” she screamed as she untangled the monster’s fingers from her hair and pulled them loose, but all she had was a handful of twigs. It was no monster at all. Her hair had been caught in the branches of a tree.

“That was scary,” she said.

But she wasn’t really scared. And she walked deeper and deeper into the forest looking for the real monster.

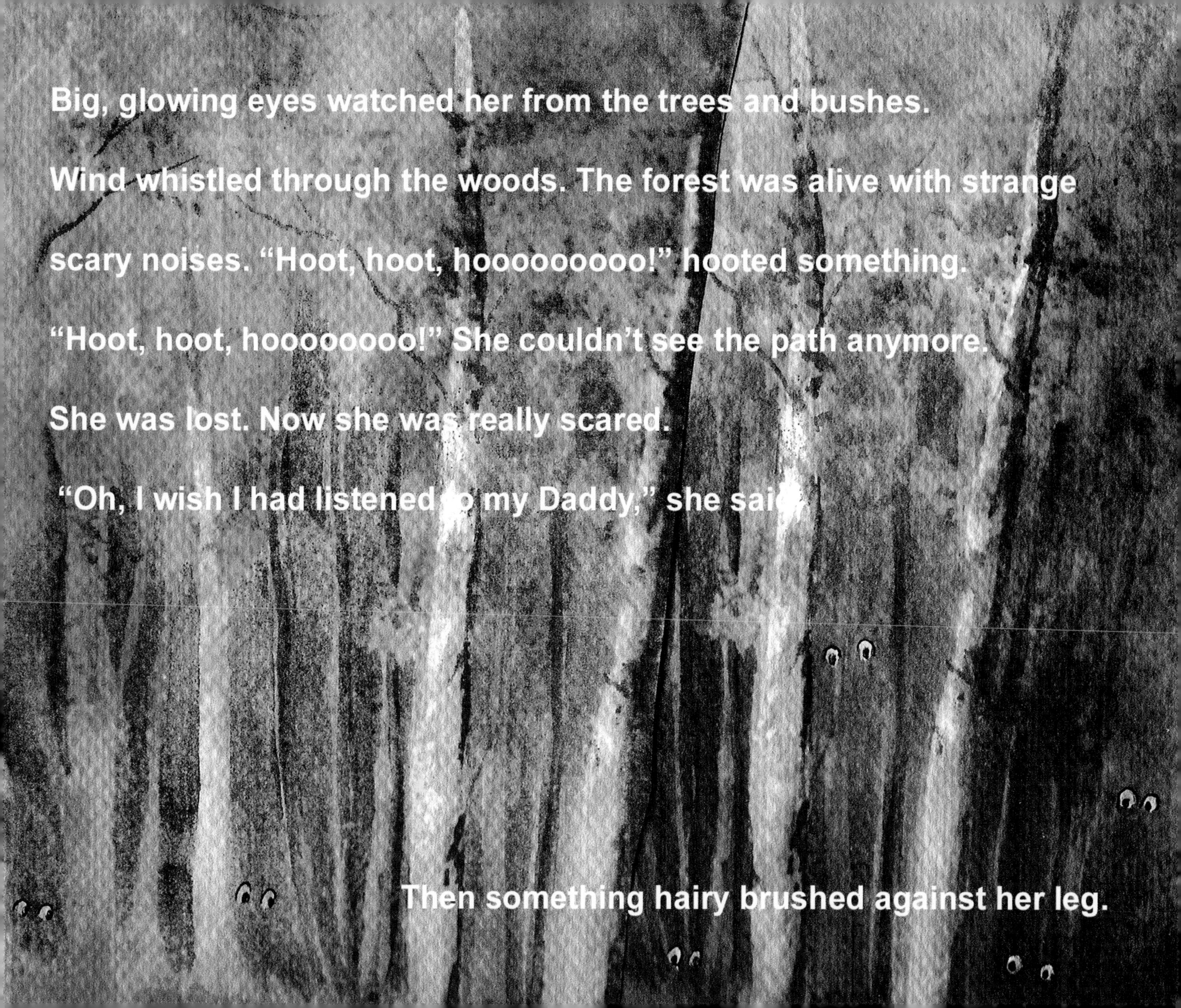

Big, glowing eyes watched her from the trees and bushes.

Wind whistled through the woods. The forest was alive with strange

scary noises. “Hoot, hoot, hoooooooooo!” hooted something.

“Hoot, hoot, hoooooooo!” She couldn’t see the path anymore.

She was lost. Now she was really scared.

“Oh, I wish I had listened to my Daddy,” she said.

Then something hairy brushed against her leg.

"Oh!" she screamed. The monster purred and jumped in her arms and licked her cheek. It was Midnight, her cat! It had followed her. "Go home! Shoo! If the monsters catch you they will eat you!" Midnight obeyed and disappeared into the darkness.

Soon she came to a hidden cottage. A light shone in a window.
She tiptoed over and peeked in.

Suddenly, big hairy hands

full of claws, grabbed he

and swooped her up!

“What have we here, dinner?” a voice roared so loud it shook the ground like thunder.

She had found the monster. It had scary, jagged teeth and hot breath that burned her eyes.

“Grrrr, I bet you’ll taste real good,” it growled, licking its lips with a big, fiery red tongue.

She kicked at the hairy beast, but it just roared with laughter. “Aren’t you a tough little bird,” it snarled, teeth gleaming in the light.

“Put me down,” she screamed, “your breath is awful!”

The monster carried her kicking and screaming into the cottage.

“Look what I caught for supper,” he roared. “She doesn’t have much meat on her, but she’ll flavor the stew nicely.”

“You better not eat me you ugly monster,” she screamed, “or I’ll give you the worst tummy ache you ever had!”

She tried to act brave, but she was really scared.

“Ho, ho, ho,” he laughed as he swung her over a big pot cooking in the fire.

“Into the stew you go!”

"Put that little girl down, Clive," said his wife. "You're scaring her."

The monster put her down as ordered.

"Oh, Maudie, I was just having a little fun," he said.

"You mean you're not going to eat me?" the girl asked her.

"Land sakes, no child. All we eat are the vegetables we grow in our garden, and nuts and berries from the forest."

"You don't eat people?" she said again in amazement.

"No. That's just an old story meant to scare children."

"Then why does everyone say monsters eat people?"

"People talk a lot of silly nonsense," she answered sadly, "and you don't help any," she said, shaking her spoon at her husband.

"Oh, I'm sorry, little girl," he said. "I was only playing."

Just then the door opened and a little boy monster came in.

“Look, Rolf,” said his mother, “we have company.”

“Hi, my name is Gerta,” she said.

“Hi, Gerta, want to play with me?” Rolf said.

“Okay,” she said, and they played on the swings in his back yard.

"You don't look like the monsters I've heard stories about," said Gerta.

"Like what?"

"Your hair isn't all matted and smelly," she said. "It's clean and neat."

"I take a bath every night and comb my hair every morning. Don't you?"

"And your fingernails aren't long and dirty, and your teeth aren't yellow."

"That's because I trim my nails and I brush my teeth after every meal."

"Where do you go to school?" asked Gerta.

"I'm home schooled," said Rolf. "Monsters aren't welcome in the village school."

"Why not?" she asked.

"Maybe it's because we look different. Once I was playing at the edge of the fores

Children in the meadow saw me and screamed. I was scared."

"I'm sorry," said Gerta.

"I don't have any friends," said Rolf. "Would you be my friend, Gerta?"

"Yes," she answered, and they played together all morning.

Soon it was time for lunch, a salad of fresh greens and vegetables from the monsters' garden, which Gerta helped pick.

All her life she was taught that monsters ate people and here they were eating vegetables. She couldn't get over it.

"You really don't eat people?"

"To tell you the truth," said Rolf's mother, don't think people would taste very good. Especially the mean ones."

The monster family all used their knives and forks properly and wiped the corners of their mouths with their napkins. Only Rolf chewed with his mouth open.

"Rolf! We have a guest. You must mind your manners," said his mother.

"Sorry, Mother," he said.

"Can Rolf come to my house for supper?" asked Gerta.

His parents agreed, and even though they trusted Gerta, they were worried.

"If you get scared, you come home right away," said Rolf's father at the edge of the forest. He kissed Rolf goodbye and watched as they walked across the meadow.

The meadow looked peaceful, but Rolf's father knew the village was scary. Monsters were safer here in the forest. It was their home.

Children playing in the meadow, saw them and ran screaming into the village, “Run, run, a monster’s coming!”, and hid in doorways.

Gerta and Rolf walked through the empty streets holding hands.

"Don't be afraid, Rolf," she whispered. People peeked out from behind curtains as they passed. "Is that a monster from the haunted glen?" asked a shopkeeper.

"But his hair isn't matted. It's neatly combed.... and his nails aren't long and dirty... and his teeth aren't yellow."

One by one, the villagers came out and gazed in wonder at the little monster as he and Gerta walked by.

Gerta's parents were sitting at the kitchen table when she walked in.

"Guess what, Mommy and Daddy? I have a new friend."

"That's nice, dear," they said. Rolf walked in behind her.

Gerta's parents screamed and cowered in a corner.

“Don’t be afraid,” Gerta said.

“What have you done?” cried her mother. “He’ll eat us.”

“And crunch our bones,” whimpered her father. “Oooooo!”

“No, he won’t,” said Gerta. “He’s just a little monster.”

“Little monsters have big appetites,” he said. “Oooooo!”

“Monsters don’t eat people,” Gerta assured them, “only vegetables.”

“His hair isn’t matted and dirty,” said her mother, astonished.

“No, he washes his face and combs his hair just like I do,” said Gerta. “And he brushes his teeth after eating, just like I do. He’s just like me, only hairy.”

“Very hairy,” said her mother.

“Incredibly hairy,” said her father.

Gerta's mother and father stared and stared. They had never seen a monster before. He seemed no different from their little girl. Except for the hair. And the teeth... And the claws... But they were clean and neatly trimmed.

"Would you like some lemonade?" asked Gerta's mother.

"Yes, thank you," said Rolf.

"We're having macaroni and cheese for supper," said Gerta's mother. "Would you like to stay and eat with us?"

"Yes, thank you, but I have to wash my hands and face first."

"Oh, my," said Gerta's father. "A little monster with manners."

After supper, they played on her swings, laughing as they swung back and forth.

Her parents watched from a window. “He seems like a nice little monster,” she sai

“Little monsters grow up into big monsters,” Gerta’s father said.

Her mother glared at him.“Sometimes you are very scary,” she said.

In her backyard, Gerta and Rolf laughed and played happily into the evening.

Soon after, a calm settled over the valley, and the villagers couldn't remembe
... why they were ever afraid of that nice family of monsters.
The En
J. Koji